the hens

the goat

the sheep and lamb

the cow and calf

the bees

the goose

Learning Points

●

Farms and farm animals fascinate young children.
Your child will enjoy sharing *Joe and the Farm Goose*
with you again and again.

●

Encourage your child to talk about the animals he or she has
seen. What were they doing? What sounds do they make?

●

Children love to recognise baby animals.
See if your child knows what the animals are called.

●

Encourage your child to turn the pages and tell you a
story of the farm visit.

●

Use our questions as a talkabout starting point,
and then think of questions of your own.

●

Can your child find the inquisitive goose throughout
the book?

A catalogue record for this book is available from the British Library

Published by Ladybird Books Ltd Loughborough Leicestershire UK
Ladybird Books is a subsidiary of the Penguin Group of companies

Illustrations © Jakki Wood MCMXCV
© LADYBIRD BOOKS LTD MCMXCV
This edition MCMXCVI
LADYBIRD and the device of a Ladybird are trademarks of Ladybird Books Ltd

Joe
and the
Farm Goose

by Geraldine Taylor *and* Jill Harker
illustrated by Jakki Wood

Ladybird

Mum and Dad, Sally and Ben and
little Joe arrived at Manor Farm.

"I want to go this way," said Sally.
A friendly goose did, too!

Dad lifted Ben up to see the cows in the field.

Joe was too little to look over the
hedge, so he peeped under it.
The goose did, too.

Everyone wanted to see the pigs.

Joe was too small to look over the
gate, so he peeped through it.
The goose did, too.

"Keep back from the tractor!"
said Mum. "What a noise."

In a quiet corner, Joe, Dad and
the goose found a duck and three
fluffy ducklings.

Sally and Ben stayed close to Dad
and watched the tractor.

Joe and the goose stayed close to Mum and found some treasure.

In the big barn, Mum and Dad and
Sally and Ben looked up high
and saw some hens.

Joe looked down low and saw some
tiny mice. The goose did, too.

One of the horses in the yard had
a baby foal. Joe peeped out from
behind Mum...

The goose did, too!

Then it was time to eat…

Joe didn't want to sit at the picnic table, he wanted to sit on the grass. The goose did, too.

In the orchard there were beehives
and a goat. "Look at those apples
up there," said Dad.

But all Joe and the goose could see
were Dad's knees – and the goat.

Joe couldn't reach the apples in the orchard – but the goose could.

Sally and Ben and Joe picked lots of strawberries. Perhaps the goose didn't like strawberries.

The farm visit was almost over.
"What an exciting day," said Dad.

Ben and Sally thought so, too –
but little Joe was asleep.

Goodbye farm. Goodbye goose…

It's our bedtime, too!

Did you find all these things?

pig and piglets

the horse and foal

the tractor

the cat

the ducks

the donkey